Get to Bed!

By Catherine Ann Russell

Illustrated by Morgan Grace Quist

Special thanks to Rachel Ann Harding,
editing consultant

Beautiful Children Stories for All Ages

Percent profit proceeds going to emergency famine relief around the world.
Find out more at www.spikeproductions.com/basketfulreliefproject

Another day draws to a close
At the Bouncing Baby Barn.
A homestead to goats and chickens
And many ducks on a farm.

A final burst of the sun's rays
Bathe the sky in dazzling displays.
Pink and orange and red and blue
Paint the sky in light and hue.

The stars twinkle in the evening sky
As nighttime falls.
The goats in the field will soon scamper
Off to their stalls.

But which goat is this do I see,
Staying behind in the field?
Why It's my friend, Big-Belly Bob
Who is unwilling to yield.

"Bob, Get Going!"

And with my keen urging
Bob kicks his heels in delight
Without too much of a fight.
To trot off back home to the barn
With the other goats on the farm.

The chickens start tucking
Themselves in for the night.
Some last bit of preening
In the sprawling twilight.

The moon rises and
Is enough to entrance.

It seems all is well
At this beautiful ranch.

Yet, what could this be?
Are these ducks that I see?

"What are you doing out?
Do I have to shout?"

But the ducks
didn't hear

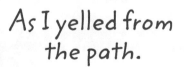

As I yelled from
the path.

They were quacking

And splashing,
In their evening bath.

Well, at least the goats
Are now ready for bed.
Before they tuck in
They'll have dinner instead.

Chickens, you're still not ready
To roost?
"Get to bed now! Do you need
A boost?"

Oh! And these ducks
Are still swimming about?
"Get to bed now
Or you're in trouble no doubt!"

Surely by now

The goats are all sleeping.

"Well! Who is this?

You are all still eating?"

Where is my goat, Meagan?
She won't tease!
"Will you go straight to bed
Pretty please?"

Meagan looked at me
And winked.
As if to say, "sure!"
But not meaning it
I think.

"It's really very late.
Is anyone asleep?"

The chickens on their roost cluck, "Nope."

The goats in their stall all bleat, "Nope."

The ducks who are still out quack, "Nope."

The moon and stars
Are too beautiful,
I sigh.
For fur-ed or feathered friends
To get some
Shut-eye.

I still need to get
the ducks inside.
I'll have to be stern --
Bedtime is nigh.

"Come on you guys please be good
To me.
Ducks, get to bed by the count
Of three!"

To my count of, "One … Two … Three!"
They tucked in their nests
Quite contentedly.

At last,

All are in bed

And safe from harm.

All is well at the

Bouncing Baby Barn.

"Good night!" Hooted an owl
Looking down from a tree.
With a start I gazed up
Just as he greeted me.

"Hi Mr. Owl,
Anything else to say?"
"Only that soon
It will dawn a new day!"

And with that he winked his eye,
Flew into the eastern sky,

Lit up in hues of violet and blue
I thought to myself, it's my bedtime too!

As I tucked myself in
For a short nap,
My round kitty, Misty
Jumped in my lap.

I stroked her fur, while she began to purr,
I thought to myself, How happy am I
And life is a treat!
With thoughts of the Bouncing Baby Barn
I fell fast asleep.

Good Night!

Basketful Relief Project

@2019 Basketful Relief Project

Get to Bed!

www.spikeproductions.com/basketfulreliefproject

The Author

Catherine Russell is a videographer who lives in Lyons, CO on a hobby farm with her husband, Ed and several fun farm animals, including two burros named Nikki and Norman. Not only does Catherine enjoy walking with goats in the hills around her home, she desires to help fight world hunger and has founded The Basketful Relief Project, working with collaborators of all talents to publish beautiful children's books (print and video), with percent profit proceeds going to emergency famine relief organizations.

The Illustrator

Morgan Grace Quist is a nurse and artist who lives in the mountains of Colorado. She grew up adventuring in the outdoors: kayaking down rivers, pitching tents in the woods, climbing tall mountains, and catching lizards on the trails. The beauty of the natural world heavily influences her artistic pieces, and you'll often find her lost in the Colorado landscape with a paintbrush in hand.